Based on the original screenplay by Elise Allen
Adapted by Justine Fontes
Illustrations by Rita Lichtwardt, Carrie Perlow, Taia Morley, Christian Musselman

Special thanks to: Vicki Jaeger, Monica Okazaki, Ann McNeill, Emily Kelly, Sharon Woloszyk, Julia Phelps, Tanya Mann, Rob Hudnut, Tiffany J. Shuttleworth, Gabrielle Miles, M. Elizabeth Hughes, Lily Martinez, and Walter P. Martishius

Reader's Digest Children's Books®

New York, New York • Montréal, Québec • Bath, United Kingdom

Barbie's beach house sizzled with excitement as she and her sisters packed for a trip to New York City for "the perfect Christmas!"

Skipper planned to podcast a friend's concert. Stacie would skate in Rockefeller Center. Barbie had front-row seats to a Broadway show! And Chelsea longed to feed sea lions at the zoo.

But their flight was forced to land in snowy Minnesota—not Manhattan!

Stacie fretted. "We won't arrive today?"

Skipper sighed. "If the storm's really bad, we won't reach New York at all."

Chelsea exclaimed, "But we have to!"

Barbie was determined, and rented a car to drive to a larger airport.

But the sisters wound up lost in the snow. Finally, they found an open inn.

"Hello-ho-ho!" pretty innkeeper Christie Clauson greeted the girls. "You're right on time!"

"For what?" Skipper wondered.

"The greatest day of the year!" Christie exclaimed. The Tannenbaum Inn sparkled with Christmas spirit.

That night, Barbie heard a beautiful song. She was surprised to find the singer was her sister, Skipper! Barbie exclaimed, "That was amazing!"

Skipper admitted, "It's something I kind of wrote."

Right away, Barbie gave Skipper advice about her song. But Skipper said, "I'm not a baby! I don't need you to jump in and do everything for me." She wanted to do something on her own, without Barbie's help.

The next morning, Skipper checked the weather and moaned, "We won't be in New York for Christmas!"

Chelsea worried Santa wouldn't find them. So Barbie suggested hanging their stockings on the windowsill. Then she noticed...reindeer! Chelsea spotted eight reindeer, too. One leaped so high he seemed to fly!

TRAVEL WARNING: SNOW SNOW SNO

Malibu

NYC

"Come on!" Chelsea shouted. "Let's go see!"

Instead of reindeer, the girls found dogs learning tricks. Christie explained, "Every year we train shelter dogs to play Santa's reindeer in our Canine Christmas." The dogs would even wear antlers!

One pooch pulled Chelsea on a wild ride that ended at a barn surrounded by real reindeer! What could be inside?

The sisters couldn't resist peeking inside. They found the barn packed with presents! Chelsea quickly concluded it must belong to Santa Claus.

But skeptical Skipper recalled Christie saying the Tannenbaum Inn always conducted a big toy drive. Stacie suggested heading back to the inn for hot cocoa.

On the way back, Skipper heard a cool Christmas carol coming from a garage. Inside she met a cute guitarist named Brian who knew her "vlog."

Brian's band really needed a singer. So Barbie suggested, "Podcast Brian's band from the hotel tonight. And you can sing your song!" She gushed on, "Christie can spread the word around town! We'll make a stage right outside and serve..."

Skipper knew Barbie wanted to help, but for once she wanted to do everything on her own, without Barbie taking over. "If I do this," she said, "I want to do it. I don't want it to be a Barbie thing."

Barbie agreed. "Deal. I'll keep totally out of it."

Since Skipper wouldn't let anyone help, she soon felt overwhelmed. Skipper snapped at Chelsea, who ran off alone!

Skipper regretted her mistake, "We have to find her! We're sisters. We work together. We always should."

Barbie, Skipper, and Stacie headed out to find Chelsea.

Finally, the sisters found Chelsea near the barn visiting the reindeer. The sisters were reunited, but with only one hour to go, would they be able to make the Christmas show happen?

Suddenly, the girls heard bells and a "ho-ho-ho." They saw sleigh tracks leading to the barn. And inside, all the gifts were gone, leaving a perfect "stage"!

"Santa took them!" Chelsea concluded, about the gifts. "And he left a present—the perfect stage!"

The show felt like Christmas magic—especially when the sisters sang Skipper's song with new lyrics, "It's a perfect Christmas, 'cuz I'm with you." No matter where the sisters were, it was a perfect Christmas—as long as they were together.